BILINGUAL EDUCATION

THE STORY OF MAH
DAB NEEG HAIS TXOG MAJ
A Hmong "Romeo and Juliet" Folktale

Retold by
Rosalie Giacchino-Baker, Ph.D.

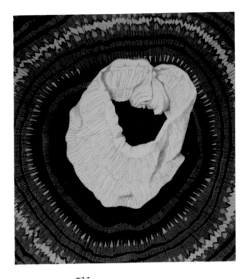

Illustrated by
Lillian Shao

Bilingual Edition: Hmong/English

Pacific Asia Press

Text copyright © Rosalie Giacchino-Baker and
Ecoles Sans Frontières, 1995.
Published by:
Pacific Asia Press
A Greenshower Corporation
10937 Klingerman St., S. El Monte, California, 91733
Tel: (818) 575-1000   FAX: (818)859-3136

First published in 1995 in
Stories from Laos.
Folktales and Cultures of the Lao, Hmong, Khammu, and Iu-Mien.
Rosalie Giacchino-Baker, Editor.

This edition of The Story of Mah. A Hmong "Romeo and Juliet" Folktale
first published in 1997.

Printed in Taiwan

Library of Congress catalog Card Number:
96-72464

Library of Congress cataloging-in Publication Data:
The Story of Mah. A Hmong "Romeo and Juliet" Folktale
retold by Rosalie Giacchino-Baker
illustrated by Lillian Shao
p.cm
Summary: One illustrated tale, map of Lao People's Democratic Republic
bilingual format: English/Hmong

ISBN: 1-879600-98-6
1. Folklore— Laos—Juvenile Literature
[1. Folklore—Laos.]
I. Giacchino-Baker, Rosalie.
II. Title.
III. Title: The Story of Mah. A Hmong "Romeo and Juliet" Folktale

Distributed by

Multicultural Distributing Center
A Greenshower Corporation
P.O. Box 4321
Covina, CA 91723 USA
1-800-LEP-HELP

We Deliver Learning

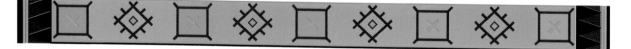

This book is dedicated to Hmong women in Laos and in the United States whose strength and courage enable their families to survive and thrive.

With special thanks to

Jeane and Tiffo Chen

John, Michael, and Sarah Baker
and Fred Baker

for their loving support of our work

nce there was a beautiful Hmong girl named Mah who was very intelligent and hard-working. Mah lived in the mountains of northern Laos in a village that was surrounded by forests.

Ntuj thaum ub muaj ib leej ntxhais Hmoob npe hu ua Maj, zoo nkauj, ntse thiab nquag heev. Maj nyob rau hauv ib lub zos hauj sab plawv zoov nuj txeeg suam toj roob hauv pes Los Tsuas qaum teb.

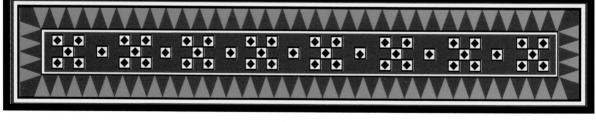

ne day as she was walking in the forest, she saw some unusual plants. She looked at them carefully and decided to take a few of them back to her village.

Muaj ib hnub thaum Maj sam sim ncig txog ib lub hav zoov, nws tau pom ib cov ntsuag ntoo txawv. Nws ua tib zoo saib tseeb tseeb, thiab txiav txim coj ob peb tug los tsev.

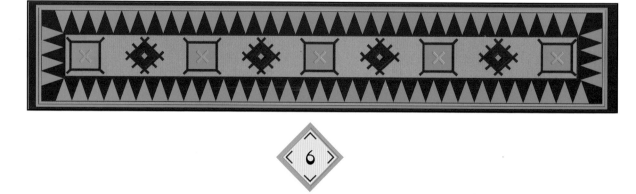

hen she got home, she made yarn from the plant and wove the yarn to make cloth. Mah's mother was curious about her daughter's work. She asked: "What are you going to do with that cloth?"
"I'm not sure," answered Mah. "Maybe we can use it as a blanket during the winter."

Thaum nws los poob tse lawd, nws muab cov ntoo laws tawv los ua

ntuag, muab cov ntuag qwv ua xov, muab xov ntos ua tau ib chaws ntaub.
     Maj niam zoo siab txog tus ntxhais tes num heev. Nws thiaj nug tias:
"Koj yuav siv chaws ntaub kod ua dab tsi ?"
     "Kuv paub tsis tau meej," Maj teb. "Tej zaum peb muab xaws ua ib daig pam vov thaum caij ntuj tsaug ."

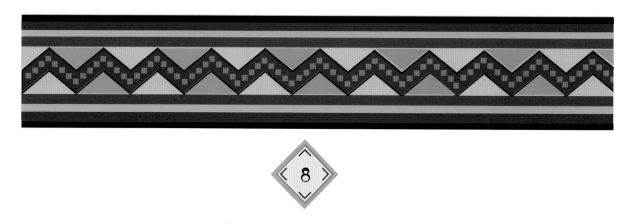

he next day, Mah went into the forest again to get more of the strange plants. On the way back to her village, she met a young man who asked if he could walk her home.

"Hi, my name is Leu Xeng," said the young man. "I live in a village north of this mountain. Can I help you carry those plants? What are you going to do with them?"

"Nice to meet you," said Mah shyly as she handed him her basket. "Yesterday I wove some cloth from this plant. I came to get more plants today." "Oh, so you're talented as well as beautiful," continued Leu Xeng. Mah lowered her eyes and smiled happily in response.

Hnub tom qab, Maj rov mus tom hav zoov muab hom ntoo txawv hais ntxiv. Thaum sam sim rov los tsev, Maj ntsib ib leeg hluas, tus hluas nug saib nws sawm puas nyog nrog Maj ua ke.

" Kuv npe hu ua Lawj Xeeb," tus hluas hais. "Kuv nyob lub zos sab pem toj qhov lub tw roob no mus kawg. Kuv pab nqa koj cov ntoo puas tau ? Koj coj ntoo mus ua dab tsi ?"

"Zoo siab qhov ntsib koj" Maj hais nyuag txaj muag tsawv, thooj txhij ntawd cev nws lub kawd rau Lawj Xeeb. "Nag hmo kuv muab cov ntoo no ntos ua tau ntaub. Hnub no kuv thiaj rov tuaj muab ntxiv." "Oh, koj lub tsev yid phim lub cev qhov zoo nkauj kawg yuam," Lawj Xeeb hais ntxiv. Maj dauv muag lawv ua laj muam ntsia thiab teb luag nyav zoo siab hlo.

< 10 >

hen they reached Mah's house, Leu Xeng admired the cloth that Mah had made. Leu Xeng found, however, that his eyes were on Mah much more than on her cloth. Before long, the young man realized that he was in love with this girl he had barely met.

When it was time to return home, he asked, "May I come to see you again tomorrow?"

"Yes, I'd like that," answered Mah softly. She thought that Leu Xeng was very good looking, and she secretly hoped he would come back often.

Time passed. The two young people saw each other as often as they could.

Thaum nkawd mus txog tom Maj tsev, Lawj Xeeb qhuas txog cov ntaub

Maj ua tau. Txawm li cas los, Lawj Xeeb ob lub qhov muag zas rau Maj tshaj ntsia Maj cov ntaub. Tsis ntev, tus hluas xeev tias nws thiab tus ntxhais nyuam qhuav ntsib muaj kev sib hlub lawm .

Txog caij rov mus tsev, nws thiaj nug tias, "Tag kis kuv rov tuaj ntsib koj puas tau ?"

"Tau, kuv nyiam qhov ntawd ," Maj teb mos nyoos. Nws xav Lawj Xeeb zoo nraug heev, thiab cia siab twj ywm tias kheev Lawj Xeeb tuaj tsis so.

Caij nyoog dhau zus. Ob tug hluas sib cuag ntxug zus.

< 12 >

ne day, while Mah was weaving, her mother sat next to her and said, "Mah, we have arranged for you to marry a young man from a good family."

"But I love Leu Xeng," said Mah who knew in her heart that her love for Leu Xeng was now impossible.

Muaj ib hnub, thaum Maj sam sim ua ntos, nws niam zaum ib sab thiab hais tias, "Maj, peb npaj kom koj yuav ib tug hluas hauv ib tse neeg muaj txiag lawm ."

" Tab sis kuv twb nyiam Lawj Xeeb lawm ne," Maj teb li twb paub hauv nruab siab lawm tias nws cog kev sib hlub nrog Lawj Xeeb khov ua cas tsis tau lawd.

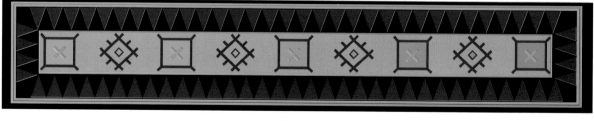

he next day Mah tearfully told Leu Xeng, "We must say good-bye. I have to marry someone else."

When Mah's mother saw the young people talking to each other, she hurried over to where they were standing. "Leu Xeng," she said, "you can't come to visit Mah anymore. She'll be getting married soon."

Leu Xeng didn't know what to say. He waved good-bye and walked back to his village.

Hnub tom qab Maj hais ua kua muag poob dawb vog rau Lawj Xeeb

tias, "Wb yuav tau sib ncaim. Kuv yuav tsum mus yuav dua lwm tus."

Thaum Maj niam pom ob tug hluas sib hais, nws ceev nrooj tuaj rau ntawm qhov chaw nkawd sawv.

"Lawj Xeeb," Maj niam hais, "koj tuaj xyuas tsis tau Maj lawm nawb. Nws yuav mus yuav txiv sai sai no."

Lawj Xeeb tsis paub yuav hais li cas. Nws ua yam tes " Nyob mog" thiab rov ncaj nraim rau tom tsev lawm.

eu Xeng was so sad that he became very sick. His father wanted to help him, but Leu Xeng didn't tell his father what was wrong.

The village shaman tried to heal him, but Leu Xeng decided that he wanted to leave this world. Everyone in his village grieved when he died.

L awj Xeeb tu siab heev ces ua rau nws tau mob tau nkeeg hnyav.   Nws

txiv yeem pab, tab sis Lawj Xeeb tsis qhia saib nws tus mob yog mob dab tsi.

Tus txiv neeb hauv zos cawm kawg txuj, tab sis Lawj Xeeb ua siab tawm kom dhau lub ntiaj teb no mus. Lawj Xeeb txoj kev tuag, ua zej zog sawv daws quaj txhua.

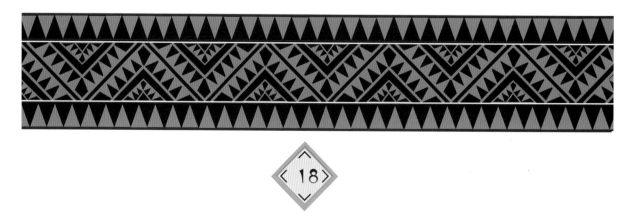

 friend went immediately to tell Mah about Leu Xeng's death. When Mah heard the news, she sobbed and said," If we can't love each other in this world, we'll have to meet in another world."

Ib leeg phooj ywg khiav kub taws ntsos mus qhia Maj tias Lawj Xeeb

tuag lawm. Thaum Maj hnov dheev lub moo ploj, nws tsa suab hlo quaj tias, "Sib hlub nyob ntiaj teb no tsis sib tau los tseg, wb mam yuj xeeb lias mus sib ntsib lawm lwm lub ntuj ."

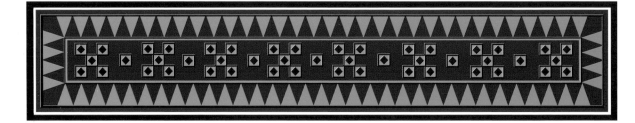

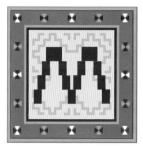 ah walked slowly and sadly into the forest. She decided that she didn't want to live without Leu Xeng who had died because of her.

Maj ntsej muag ntshaus ntshov rhais ruam qeeb tsawv tu siab nrho dua tom hav zoov lawm. Nws ua siab tias Lawj Xeeb ploj tuag vim nws hiam, yog tsis muaj Lawj Xeeb, tsis tas ua neeg nyob.

hat night Mah's mother went into the forest to look for her daughter who had not returned to the village. When she found Mah's body, she cried and asked, "How could you do it? It's all my fault." She buried Mah near Leu Xeng so the two of them could be together forever.

Hmo ntawd tsis los tsev, Maj niam thiaj mus nrhiav nws tus ntxhais tom hav zoov. Thaum nrhiav tau Maj cev ntaj ntsug tuag zooj nyoos, leej niad quaj nyiav tias, "Me ntxhais cas thiaj ua li no ? Kuv yog tus txhaum os ." Nws muab Maj coj mus faus nrog Lawj Xeeb ua txig xwv nkawd tau nyob ua ke mus ib txhis.

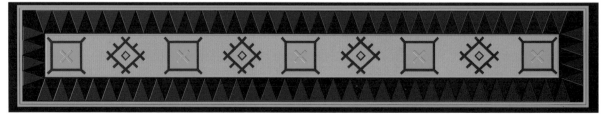

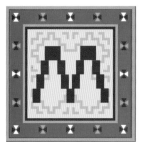 any months passed. A hemp plant began to grow on Mah's grave. The softness of the plant made Mah's mother think of her daughter.
She called the plant Mah and replanted in her garden.

Ntau lub hlis tom qab. Ib tsob ntoo tuaj rau saum Maj lub ntxa. Tej

nplooj mos nyoos ntsuab xiab ua rau leej niad nco nws tus ntxhais. Nws thiaj tis tsob ntoo npe hu ua Maj thiab coj los cog rau hauv nws lub vaj.

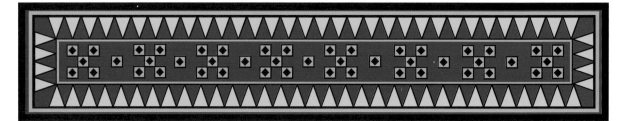

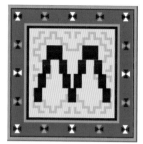 ore weeks and months passed, and the Mah plant grew and spread. When the plants were ready, the mother stripped their bark so they could be woven into cloth. She then used the cloth to make a beautiful skirt. Since that day, all Hmong mothers make special skirts out of hemp for their daughters' weddings.

Ntau lis piam ntau hlis los mus, tsob Maj loj hlob thiab huam ntxoov nyes. Thaum hlob kawg txhav leej niad laws cov tawv los ua ntuag qwv ua xov ntos ua ntaub. Tas ntawd muab ntaub xaws ua tau tiab zoo nkauj heev.

Txij ntawd los, txhua leej niam tsev Hmoob thiaj paub ua maj ua ntuag siv ntaub Maj xaws tiab npaj ntim tej ntxhais zam saum kev ua txij ua nkawm .

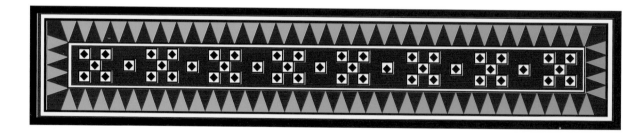

Rosalie Giacchino-Baker

Dr. Giacchino-Baker is an Associate Professor of Education at California State University, San Bernardino where her areas of specialization include second language and multicultural education. She has taught French, Spanish, and English as a Second Language in American high schools and universities. Her international experiences include living and working in France, England, Belize, Micronesia, and Thailand. During the 1993-94 school year she lived in the Lao People's Democratic Republic where she studied the cultures and educational systems of the country. She has written many articles, as well as the following books about Laos: *Stories from Laos. Folktales and Cultures of the Lao, Hmong,Khammu, and Iu-Mien; Making Connections with Hmong Culture. A Teacher's Resource Book of Thematic Classroom Activities that Promote Intercultural Understanding; Making Connections with the Story of Mah. A Teacher's Resource Book of Thematic Classroom Activities that Promote Intercultural Understanding.* [All published by Pacific Asia Press]

Lillian Shao

Lillian Shao is a talented artist whose training in the great Chinese art of calligraphy began at the age of six. Instructed by her grandfather in her native country of Taiwan, she learned many calligraphy styles, including those of the third century, B.C. and fourth century, A.D.. These early skills formed the foundation for her artistic development.

Today Ms. Shao's work is infused with many influences from both East and West. Her compositions include elements of Art Deco, Greek mythology, and Chinese poetry. Contemporary design and ancient art form combine to create her distinctive style.

Ms. Shao has spent many hours studying the textiles and folk art of the Hmong and working with Hmong consultants. Her illustrations for *The Story of Mah* are authentic and creative depictions of Hmong culture.

Ms. Shao received her M.A. from California State University, Los Angeles.

Educational Team

Kathy Felts and Tina Bacon worked closely on the design and production of this book. As experts in Teaching English to Speakers of Other Languages, they offered valuable suggestions on making the book attractive and user-friendly for young people and their teachers.

Kathy Felts' contributions to this book, however, extend far beyond those of advisor. She was responsible for assembling the team of writers, artists, and consultants. She has coordinated, guided, and promoted all aspects of this project.

Hmong Consultants in the United States

This book would not have been possible without the collaboration of Hmong consultants who participated in all stages of the project. In the United States the following persons reviewed and offered suggestions on both the Hmong text and illustrations: Dr. Kou Yang, Dr. Lue Vang, Ms. Ia Vang, Ms. Monique Yang, Mrs. Greenlee Yang, and Mr. Leasueday Yang.

Contributions from the Lao People's Democratic Republic

This story was collected in the province of Luang Prabang in the Lao PDR by a team from Ecoles sans Frontières (ESF), a multinational community development organization. Mr. Dang Duang Tou, a Hmong community development expert on the ESF staff, provided invaluable explanations of Hmong traditions. The three staff artists at ESF, Mr. Tongsay Phouvong Kamchay, Mr. Sakda Bopho Ampalak, and Mr. Philom Somsuthi, brought life to the original publication of "The Story of Mah" in *Stories from Laos. Folktales and Cultures of the Lao, Hmong, Khammu, and Iu-Mien.* Mr. Daniel Gelhay, then Director of Materials and Media, Ecoles sans Frontières, Vientiane, Lao PDR was the guiding force in recording and illustrating the "The Story of Mah" in *Stories from Laos* so that it could be read and appreciated around the world.